Dear Parent:
Your child's love of reading starts here!

Every child learns to read in a different way and at his or her own speed. Some go back and forth between reading levels and read favorite books again and again. Others read through each level in order. You can help your young reader improve and become more confident by encouraging his or her own interests and abilities. From books your child reads with you to the first books he or she reads alone, there are I Can Read Books for every stage of reading:

SHARED READING
Basic language, word repetition, and whimsical illustrations, ideal for sharing with your emergent reader

BEGINNING READING
Short sentences, familiar words, and simple concepts for children eager to read on their own

READING WITH HELP
Engaging stories, longer sentences, and language play for developing readers

READING ALONE
Complex plots, challenging vocabulary, and high-interest topics for the independent reader

ADVANCED READING
Short paragraphs, chapters, and exciting themes for the perfect bridge to chapter books

I Can Read Books have introduced children to the joy of reading since 1957. Featuring award-winning authors and illustrators and a fabulous cast of beloved characters, I Can Read Books set the standard for beginning readers.

A lifetime of discovery begins with the magical words "I Can Read!"

Visit www.icanread.com for information
on enriching your child's reading experience.

To my sister Steph, for all you do for kids
—B.H.

For Mel, Anne, and Meika
—G.F.

I Can Read Book® is a trademark of HarperCollins Publishers.

Clark the Shark and the Big Book Report
Copyright © 2017 by HarperCollins Publishers
All rights reserved. Manufactured in China.
No part of this book may be used or reproduced in any manner whatsoever without written permission except in the case of brief quotations embodied in critical articles and reviews. For information address HarperCollins Children's Books, a division of HarperCollins Publishers, 195 Broadway, New York, NY 10007.
www.icanread.com

Library of Congress Control Number: 2016952351
ISBN 978-0-06-227913-2 (trade bdg.) — ISBN 978-0-06-227912-5 (pbk.)

Typography by Erica De Chavez

17 18 19 20 21 SCP 10 9 8 7 6 5 4 3 2 1   ❖   First Edition

I Can Read!

BEGINNING READING 1

CLARK THE SHARK
AND THE BIG BOOK REPORT

WRITTEN BY **BRUCE HALE**   ILLUSTRATED BY **GUY FRANCIS**

"Tomorrow is Book Report Day,"
said Mrs. Inkydink.

"Is everybody ready?"

Only a few flippers went up.

"I'm nervous," said Benny Blowfish.

"I'm scared," said Ella Jellyfish.

"I can't wait!" said Clark the Shark.

"If you're worried about speaking,"
said Mrs. Inkydink, "just remember:
be bold, be smart,
and speak from the heart."

"I'm not worried!" said Clark, laughing.

"Mine will be the best report ever!"

At recess, Joey Mackerel asked,
"Aren't you nervous about
talking in front of the class?"

"Easy-peasy!" said Clark.

"I know my book

like the back of my flipper!"

At lunch, Clark made up
a joke for his report.

Kenny Ahi laughed so hard
milk squirted from his gills!

That night, Clark tried out his report on his family. They laughed and clapped.

Clark even made a fancy poster

of the book cover,

with a little help from Mom.

On the way to school, Joey asked,

"Are you ready?"

"I'm so ready," said Clark,

"they should film my report.

It'll be perfect!"

All through their morning lessons,

Clark wriggled and wiggled.

He couldn't wait to give his report.

Finally the time came.

"Who will go first?"

asked Mrs. Inkydink.

Nobody spoke. Nobody but Clark.

"Me, me, me!" he said.

"Pick me!"

Clark got up and told his joke:
"What do frog princes eat with
their hamburgers?"

"French flies!" Clark said.

Everybody cracked up.

And then . . . it happened.

Clark forgot what came next.

His mind was as empty as a seashell.

"Uh," he said. "Um . . ."

Clark had a brain freeze.

He wanted to shrink and disappear.

Clark was totally tongue-tied.

His friends cheered him on.

"You can do it, Clark," said Joey.

Clark smacked his face

and stood on his head.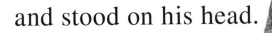

But the words
wouldn't shake loose.

"Be bold, be smart,"

said Mrs. Inkydink.

"And speak . . ."

"From the heart!" said Clark.

Suddenly his mind was clear again.

Clark went on with his book report.

Maybe it wasn't perfect,

but it *was* from the heart.

And what do you know?

His classmates loved every word.

CLARK THE SHARK'S BITE-SIZED FACTS

1 Sharks don't really go to school, but some swim *in* schools. A school is a group of fish that swims together.

2 Sharks can communicate with one another using vibrations in the water and body movements.

3 Some sharks have good memories! They can be trained to do simple tasks and remember how to do them for a long time.